ISSUES today

Obesity and Fitness

Edited by Christina Hughes

Series Editor: Cara Acred

Vol. 76

Independence Educa

First published by Independence

The Studio, High Green, Great Shelford

Cambridge CB22 5EG

England

© Independence 2013

British Library Cataloguing in Publication Data

Obesity and fitness. -- (Issues today ; 76)

1. Physical fitness--Juvenile literature. 2. Obesity--

Juvenile literature.

I. Series II. Acred, Cara editor of compilation.

613.7-dc23

ISBN-13: 978 1 86168 653 4

Acknowledgements

The publisher is grateful for permission to reproduce the following material. While every care has been taken to trace and acknowledge copyright, the publisher tenders its apology for any accidental infringement or where copyright has proved untraceable. The publisher would be pleased to come to a suitable arrangement in any such case with the rightful owner.

Chapter One: Obesity

Facts and figures on obesity © Crown Copyright 2012, *Reducing obesity and improving diet* © Crown Copyright 2013, *British people among laziest in Europe* © Nick Collins/The DailyTelegraph, *The NHS jobsworths employed to brand kids as fat* © Adam Collyer 2011, *Obese children to be put up for adoption* © Nick Collins/The DailyTelegraph, *New UK obesity centre offers surgery to teens* © independent.co.uk 2013, *Sugar and calories reduced in soft drinks* © Crown Copyright 2013, *Parents 'are scared to talk to their children about weight issues'* © ITV plc 2012.

Chapter Two: Fitness

Start active, stay active © Crown Copyright 2011, *Half of people in the UK cannot run 100 metres* © 2000-2013 YouGov plc, *Fitness training tips* © NHS Choices 2011, *'How I caught the running bug'* © NHS Choices 2012, *Zombie fitness app a runaway success for UK business* © Nesta 2012, *Outdoor fitness equipment: taking the 'play' out of the playground* © Fitness Newspaper 2013, *New research shows that healthy teenagers are happy teenagers* © PSHE Association 2012, *Young women and girls' physical activity* © Women's Sport and Fitness Foundation 2010, *American sisters, aged eight and nine, start their own fitness class* © Cara Acred/Independence Educational Publishers Ltd., *Fitness advice for wheelchair users* © NHS Choices 2012.

Illustrations on pages 4 and 17 are by Angelo Madrid. All other illustrations, including the cover, are by Don Hatcher.

Images: page 3 © Alex Raths, page 8 © StÃ©fan, page 9 © Kim Gunkel, page 13 © Gordon Warlow, pages 19, 20 & 23 © Jackie Staines, page 21 © sanja gjenero, page 26 © Percita.

Editorial by Christina Hughes and layout by Jackie Staines, on behalf of Independence Educational Publishers.

Printed in Great Britain by MWL Print Group Ltd.

Cara Acred

Cambridge

May 2013

Contents

About *ISSUES* today

ISSUES today is a series of resource books on contemporary social issues, designed for Key Stage 3 pupils and above. This series is also suitable for Scottish P7, S1 and S2 students.

Each volume contains information from a variety of sources, including government reports and statistics, newspaper and magazine articles, surveys and polls, academic research and literature from charities and lobby groups. The information has been tailored to an 11 to 14 age group; it has been rewritten and presented in a simple, straightforward and accessible format.

In addition, each **ISSUES today** title features handy tasks and assignments based on the information contained in the book, for use in class, for homework or as a revision aid.

ISSUES today can be used as a learning resource in a variety of Key Stage 3 subjects, including English, Science, History, Geography, PSHE, Citizenship, Sex and Relationships Education and Religious Education.

About this book

Obesity and Fitness is Volume 76 in the **ISSUES today** series.

'I'm not overweight, I'm just big boned' – fact or fiction? With so many myths flying around about obesity, it is important to know more about this modern day epidemic and how to start tackling the dangers of being overweight. This book explores the causes and impacts of obesity, alongside the concepts of fitness and staying healthy. With British people being classed as among the laziest in Europe and parents too scared to talk to their children about weight problems, it is vital that we confront these issues.

Obesity and Fitness offers a useful overview of the many issues involved in this topic. However, at the end of each article is a URL for the relevant organisation's website, which can be visited by pupils who want to carry out further research.

Because the information in this book is gathered from a number of different sources, pupils should think about the origin of the text and critically evaluate the information that is presented. Does the source have a particular bias or agenda? Are you being presented with facts or opinions? Do you agree with the writer?

At the end of each chapter there are two pages of activities relating to the articles and issues raised in that chapter. The 'Brainstorm' questions can be done as a group or individually after reading the articles. This should prompt some ideas and lead on to further activities. Some suggestions for such activities are given under the headings 'Oral', 'Moral dilemmas', 'Research', 'Written' and 'Design' that follow the 'Brainstorm' questions.

For more information about **ISSUES today** and its sister series, **ISSUES** (for pupils aged 14 to 18), please visit the Independence website.

www.independence.co.uk

Facts and figures on obesity

What is obesity?

'Obesity' is a term used to describe excess body fat that is associated with risks to health. Being obese can increase the risk of diseases such as type 2 diabetes, cancer and heart disease. Obesity affects people's health, their lives and the lives of their families. It also puts a large financial burden on the NHS.

Obesity figures

Obesity in England has more than tripled in the last 25 years.

The latest Health Survey for England (HSE) data shows that in England in 2010:

➤ 62.8% of adults (aged 16 or over) were overweight or obese.

➤ 30.3% of children (aged 2-15) were overweight or obese.

➤ 26.1% of all adults and 16% of all children were obese.

Recent reports suggest that, without action, 41-48% of men and 35-43% of women could be obese by 2030.

Measuring obesity

The most common way of measuring whether someone is obese is by calculating their Body Mass Index (BMI).

In adults, a BMI of 25 to 29.9 means that person is overweight, and a BMI of 30 or above means that person is obese.

In children and adolescents, BMI varies with age and sex.

BMI is the best way we have to measure how many people are obese. Certain factors such as fitness and ethnic origin can sometimes alter the relationship between BMI and body fat. If this is the case, other measurements such as waist circumference and skin fold thickness can also be collected to confirm an individual person's weight status.

Causes of obesity

Becoming overweight or obese is the result of eating more calories than needed and/or not doing enough physical activity to match the amount of calories eaten.

It is clear that reducing overall calorie intake is key to losing weight. Increasing physical activity can also be helpful in achieving weight loss and keeping a healthy body weight.

Impact of obesity

Being obese or overweight brings significant health risks. We know that, compared with a healthy weight man, an obese man is:

➤ five times more likely to develop type 2 diabetes;

➤ three times more likely to develop cancer of the colon;

➤ more than two and a half times more likely to develop high blood pressure – a major risk factor for stroke and heart disease.

An obese woman, compared with a healthy weight woman, is:

➤ almost 13 times more likely to develop type 2 diabetes;

➤ more than four times more likely to develop high blood pressure;

➤ more than three times more likely to have a heart attack.

Because of these health risks, obese and overweight people can put a significant burden on the NHS, with direct costs estimated to be £5.1 billion per year.

Advice on weight and lifestyle

You can find advice on losing weight on NHS Choices and healthy living tips on the Change4Life site.

30 April 2012

DID YOU KNOW? *BMI is calculated by dividing a person's weight measurement (in kilograms) by the square of their height (in metres).*

www.gov.uk/dh

Reducing obesity and improving diet

The latest statement from the Department of Health, concerning obesity in the UK.

Issue

In England, most people are overweight or obese. This includes 61.3% of adults and 30% of children aged between 2 and 15. People who are overweight have a higher risk of getting type 2 diabetes, heart disease and certain cancers. Excess weight can also make it more difficult for people to find and keep work, and it can affect self-esteem and mental health.

Health problems associated with being overweight or obese cost the NHS more than £5 billion every year.

By 2020, we want to see:

➢ a downward trend in the level of excess weight in adults

➢ a sustained downward trend in the level of excess weight in children.

Actions

Helping people to make healthier choices

It is important that we encourage and help people to:

➢ eat and drink more healthily

➢ be more active.

We are:

➢ giving people advice on a healthy diet and physical activity through our Change4Life programme

➢ improving labelling on food and drink to help people make healthy choices – we want a labelling system that makes it clear what is in food and drink, and we want the food and drink industry to be consistent in its approach to labelling

➢ encouraging businesses on the high street to include calorie information on their menus so that people can make healthy choices.

➢ giving people guidance on how much physical activity they should be doing.

Encouraging responsible business

Through our Public Health Responsibility Deal, businesses and organisations can make it easier for everyone - from staff to customers – to make healthier choices.

The Responsibility Deal has four networks (alcohol, food, health at work and physical activity) which all have collective pledges that businesses are encouraged to sign up to. Our actions to help people eat more healthily include:

➢ reducing ingredients (for example salt and fat) that can be harmful if people eat too much of them

➢ encouraging people to eat more fruit and vegetable to help reach their 5 a day

➢ putting calorie information on menus

➢ helping people to eat fewer calories (for example by changing the portion size or the recipe of a product).

Meeting local needs

Local councils are responsible for working with other organisations to improve the health of people living in their area. This includes making sure that the right services are in place.

We will be giving local councils a budget specifically for public health, which will allow them to provide services that meet the health needs of their local community. This could include making their own plans for helping local people who are overweight or obese, for example by providing weight loss services.

Local councils will also have health and wellbeing boards that bring together local organisations to create an environment in which people can make healthier choices.

25 March 2013

www.gov.uk

British people among laziest in Europe

Britons are among the laziest people in Europe, according to a study which found that almost two thirds of adults are putting their health at risk through a lack of exercise.

By Nick Collins, science correspondent

Only Malta and Serbia saved British people the title of the most slothful in the continent by a new study into global levels of activity.

Some 63 per cent of adults in this country are failing to meet health guidelines which recommend at least 30 minutes of moderate exercise, such as brisk walking, five times a week or 20 minutes of more vigorous activity three times a week.

Falling below this target can raise the risk of conditions like heart disease, diabetes and certain types of cancer by 20 to 30 per cent, doctors warn.

Our lethargy is double the global average and the eighth worst of the 122 countries studied, which collectively account for 89 per cent of the world's population.

Malta was the laziest country worldwide, with 72 per cent of adults classified as physically inactive, but Britain (63%) far outstretched other countries like the USA (41%), France (33%) and Greece (16%).

One third of adults across the world and four in five teenagers are physically inactive according to the study, which was based on self-reported data.

Pedro Hallal of Universidade Federal de Pelotas in Brazil, who led the study, said: 'In most countries, inactivity rises with age and is higher in women than in men. Inactivity is also increased in high-income countries.'

The study is part of a wider series on physical activity published in the latest issue of the Lancet journal.

In a separate paper, researchers from Harvard Medical School reported that lack of exercise now ranks alongside smoking and obesity in its contribution to disease.

Physical inactivity was responsible for 5.3 million of the 57 million deaths worldwide in 2008 including six to ten per cent of cases of heart disease, type 2 diabetes, breast and colon cancer, they estimated.

Professor Mark Batt, President of the UK Faculty of Sport and Exercise Medicine, said: 'Physical activity is the most prevalent modifiable risk factor for chronic disease, and this is one of the many reasons we need to work harder to promote the advantages of exercise across the country.

'Physical activity should be ingrained in daily routines and our way of life, but this is simply not the case at the moment.'

18 July 2012

Mini glossary

Lethargy – *lack of energy and feeling tired.*

The above article originally appeared in The Telegraph and is reprinted with permission. © Nick Collins/The Daily Telegraph

www.telegraph.co.uk

The NHS jobsworths employed to brand kids as fat

NHS jobsworths have produced yet another set of scare statistics, this time on 'child obesity'.

By Adam Collyer

> *NHS figures for the past year show that 19% of children in their final year of primary school were classed as obese, compared with 18.7% the previous year.*

But obesity fell to 9.4% in children going into reception, down from 9.8% the previous year.

Apart from producing a great source of copy for the media, what is the use of these statistics?

They are produced by The National Child Measurement Programme (copyright: Tony Blair 1995). This measures all school kids when they start primary school and again as they get to the end of primary school.

The purpose, according to their website, is:

'The information collected helps your local NHS provider to plan and provide better health services for the children in your area.'

In other words, they serve no purpose – unless 'health services' includes putting pressure on parents to turn their kids into anorexics.

We all know that cakes and chips are bad for our kids, don't we? And we all know that feeding our kids healthy food is a good idea. The statistics prove that – wait for it – people feed their kids cake and chips anyway.

Obviously no figures are published for the cost of all this, as NHS finances are completely opaque to the public. But the cost of this measurement programme must be quite high. The survey is, after all, measuring a million pupils every year. The survey – even without these so called 'actions' that are taken as a result of it – must run into many millions of pounds of our taxes.

One can only hope that not too many children (and their parents) are made miserable by being branded 'obese' when a fifth of kids are heavier than they are.

But mostly, really, the jobsworths who waste their lives running this programme just need to be told to get a life. We don't need their useless information, and we don't want our taxes wasted on their salaries.

They are a great example of why the NHS is crumbling.

14 December 2011

The above information is reprinted with kind permission from Adam Collyer.
© Adam Collyer 2011

www.adamcollyer.wordpress.com

Mini glossary

Jobsworth *– A person who deliberately uses their job in an unhelpful way, or enjoys using their job to make things difficult for people.*

Obese children to be put up for adoption

A couple may have their obese children removed after social services ruled they had not lost enough weight.

By Nick Collins, science correspondent

> The mother and father of seven children, six of whom are overweight, face the 'unbearable' prospect of never seeing their four youngest again if authorities act on a threat to remove them.

Three girls aged 11, five and one, and a boy aged five, are to be put up for adoption or 'fostered without contact' because their parents failed to help them slim down.

This means the parents will be unable to trace them and the family could only be reunited if the children attempt to find their family when they are grown up.

Social services warned the couple three years ago that their children would be taken away from them if they did not bring their weight under control.

The family spent two years living in a special council-funded house in which they were placed under a curfew and only three of the children were permitted to live with their parents at any one time.

But although they were placed under constant supervision and social workers observed them during meal times, no dietary rules were imposed and there was no significant improvement in the children's weight.

On Tuesday social workers informed the parents, who have been married for 20 years, of their decision to permanently remove their children.

The couple, from Dundee, are not guilty of any crime and have faced no accusations of deliberate abuse or cruelty.

Critics said the case, which is without precedent in Britain, was a serious breach of the family's human rights and exposed the worrying extent to which the State can interfere in family life.

The mother, aged 42, told the Mail on Sunday: 'They picked on us because of our size to start with and they just haven't let go, despite the fact we've done everything to lose weight and meet their demands.'

The father, aged 56, added: 'The pressure of living in the family unit would have broken anyone. We were being treated like children and cut off from the outside world. To have a social worker stand and watch you eat is intolerable.'

A Dundee City Council spokesperson said: 'The council always acts in the best interests of children, with their welfare and safety in mind.'

5 September 2011

> *The above article originally appeared in The Telegraph and is reprinted with permission. © Nick Collins/The Daily Telegraph*

www.telegraph.co.uk

New UK obesity centre offers surgery to teens

London hospital says treatment is necessary to fight epidemic among children.

By Sanchez Manning

A London hospital has set up the United Kingdom's first specialist centre offering extreme weight loss surgery for children and teenagers.

Childhood obesity rates are rising fast in the UK, with latest statistics showing that a third of children aged 10-11 in England suffer from obesity or weight issues.

In Southwark, the south London borough where Britain's first paediatric bariatric (weight-loss) surgery service is located, 40 per cent of secondary school children are classed as obese or overweight.

Ashish Desai, the surgeon who decided to set up the new centre at King's College Hospital to cater for 13- to 18-year-olds, said it was in response to what is becoming an epidemic. So far he has performed drastic weight loss procedures, mostly gastric band operations, on four teenagers.

Increasing numbers of young people in the United Kingdom are having bariatric surgery procedures that are normally carried out on adults. The National Obesity Forum estimates that up to 30 youngsters a year are travelling abroad with their parents for such treatment.

Such is the demand that hospitals in Sheffield, Leeds, Nottingham, Oxford, Cardiff and Newcastle are believed to be planning paediatric bariatric centres.

The youngest patient Mr Desai has operated on was a 13-year-old boy suffering from bone problems related to his obesity that meant he had to use a wheelchair.

According to the Indian-born physician, two of the other operations he performed are already proving to be successful.

'Two of the patients who have had long-term follow-ups of two to six months say they are extremely pleased with the results,' he said. 'They say that their attitude to food has changed completely. And now rather than going for the chips and fried food they go towards the salad.'

How does a gastric band work?

A gastric band is a soft plastic band that is fitted around the stomach to create a small pouch. The pouch has a narrow opening which leads to the rest of the stomach. Because the pouch that food enters first is so small, patients feel full after eating only a tiny amount of solid food.

The tightness of the band can be adjusted, to determine how quickly food passes into the stomach.

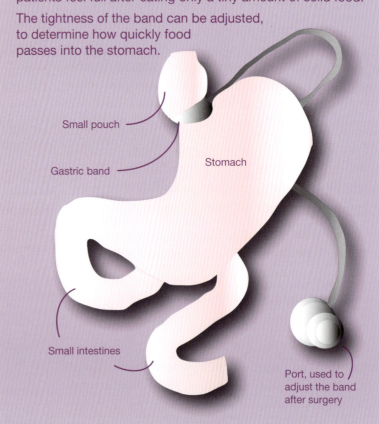

Small pouch

Gastric band

Stomach

Small intestines

Port, used to adjust the band after surgery

Mr Desai said surgery can provide a lasting solution for a wide range of obesity-related problems including diabetes, sleep apnoea and bone or liver disorders.

If patients maintain a good diet and exercise regime after having the procedure, they can typically expect to lose between 30 per cent and 50 per cent of their excess body weight.

One of Mr Desai's patients, Jayne (not her real name), had gastric band surgery in February, having an elastic band across the top end of her stomach to restrict the amount of food she can eat before feeling full. At the time of the operation she was 17, weighed 23 stone and had a body mass index (BMI) of 45.

She said: 'There are things in my life that mounted up and I used food as my comfort. I tried loads of diets but my weight was a brick wall.' In the two months after the operation she lost five stone and dropped four dress sizes.

But Mr Desai warned that weight-loss surgery is by no means a quick-fix solution to shifting the pounds – it is the last resort. He emphasised that any young people who attend his service go through an intensive six-month treatment programme with a dietician, a paediatrician and a psychologist.

After this time patients must still meet strict criteria even to be considered for the surgery, including having a BMI of at least 40 and having reached full puberty. They must further possess the 'mental maturity' to understand the implications of the operation. 'They should understand this surgery is drastic and will require lifelong commitment and changes in diet and lifestyle,' Mr Desai said.

Another important factor is the after-care the young people receive, with patients attending between ten and 12 follow-up appointments annually.

However, Mr Desai added: 'The main goal that the community and the Government need to work together to achieve is to stop this problem through prevention.'

13 May 2012

www.independent.co.uk

Mini glossary

Bariatric (weight-loss) surgery *– surgery that helps people who are dangerously overweight to lose weight. Bariatric surgery is not a quick-fix, it is a serious operation and should only be considered when all other avenues have been explored.*

Sugar and calories reduced in soft drinks

Leading soft drinks brands Lucozade, Ribena and J20 are among the latest brands to sign up to the Responsibility Deal's calorie reduction pledge as part of the government's drive to curb obesity levels.

Ribena Ready to Drink and Lucozade Energy will reduce the amount of sugar and calories they contain by up to 10%. AG Barr, producers of Irn-Bru, will reduce the calorific content across their portfolio of drinks by 5%; and J2O will launch two flavours in a new slim-line can representing a 10% calorie reduction compared with their standard 275ml bottle.

Public Health Minister Anna Soubry said:

'Being overweight and not eating well is bad for our health. To reverse the rising tide of obesity we have challenged the nation to reduce our calorie intake by five billion calories a day. On average that's just 100 calories less a day per person.

'Today's announcement will cut the calories and sugar by up to 10% in leading brands like Lucozade and Ribena. Through the Responsibility Deal we are already achieving real progress in helping people reduce the calories and salt in their diet. Overall, more than 480 companies including many leading high street brands have signed up to the Responsibility Deal.

'We are encouraged by the extra businesses which have signed up today but I want to see even more progress. All in the food industry have a part to play and I now expect companies which are not yet taking action to come forward and make pledges.'

England has some of the highest obesity rates in the developed world with 60% of adults and one third of 10 and 11 year olds being overweight or obese. The government's Obesity Call to Action outlined that consuming too many calories is at the heart of the problem and through initiatives like the Responsibility Deal Calorie Reduction pledge concerted action is needed.

Chair of the Responsibility Deal Food Network Dr Susan Jebb said:

'I'm pleased to see the soft drinks manufacturers, like GSK, AG Barr and Britvic join Coca-Cola and PepsiCo to make some very real commitments to help consumers cut down on their calories as they take control of their weight.'

'I hope we will now see others, including the out of home sector, taking a careful look at how they can build on this and come to the table with new commitments to encourage their customers to choose smaller portions and swap to lower calorie options.'

The eight new drink and food manufacturers, supermarket and catering companies which have signed up today include GlaxoSmithKline, Co-Operative Food, Burtons Biscuits, AG Barr, Britvic, Dairy Crest Lexington Catering and CH&Co. They join the 23 companies including Asda, Coca-Cola GB, Mars, Tesco and Subway that have already signed up.

22 January 2013

Four grams of sugar is equal to one teaspoon.

Next time you have a soft drink take a look at the nutrition label to see how much sugar it contains. Is it more than you thought?

www.dh.gov.uk

Parents 'are scared to talk to their children about weight issues'

Parents are worried that talking to their child about their weight will lead to an eating disorder.

A new report has found that parents are concerned that talking to their child about their weight will lead to an eating disorder.

This figure rises to 65% of parents who identify their child as being overweight or obese.

More than 1,000 parents with a child aged 5- to 16-years-old responded to the *Let's talk about weight* survey on Netmums and shared how they feel about bringing up the topic of weight with their child.

Over a third of parents (37%) feel that talking to their child about their weight might lower their self-esteem.

Despite such concerns 42% of parents have attempted to talk to their child about weight but almost half of parents who had an overweight or obese child said it was an unhelpful experience for the family.

Two thirds of parents (66%) said they'd like more support in talking to their child about weight.

This increased to 85% of parents with an overweight or obese child.

Only 32% of parents found it difficult to help their child stay healthy.

Parents with an overweight or obese child (72%) said they found it difficult to help their child to stay healthy.

Most attributed this to their child's preference for foods high in fat and sugar.

Three quarters of parents often talked to their children about what they eat but over half of these parents haven't talked to them about their weight.

2 July 2012

> 'Every parent wants the best for their child and although initially it may be a tough conversation to have, the family talking together and working together to find healthier ways of eating will lead to happier and healthier children.'
>
> *Netmums founder Siobhan Freegard*

> 'With obesity affecting a third of the UK's children, we can no longer afford for weight to be a taboo subject. It's crucial that we talk about obesity in a helpful way with a focus on the positive aspects of being healthy rather than looking good.'
>
> *Dr Paul Chadwick at Mend*

DID YOU KNOW?

According to studies, 75% of parents underestimate the size of an overweight child and 50% underestimate the size of an obese child.

Paul Gately, professor of exercise and obesity at Leeds Metropolitan University, says that this could be because 'Two thirds of adults in the UK are now classified as overweight, so our perception of what we consider the average size to be has changed.'

Source: Child obesity: why do parents let their kids get fat? *Denise Winterman, BBC News Magazine, 26 September 2012.*

www.itv.com/news

Activities

Brainstorm

1. What is obesity and how is it measured?

2. What are the effects of being obese or overweight? Think about emotional as well as physical effects.

Oral activities

3. With a partner, debate the following motion: 'Gastric band surgery is an easy-option. People should be forced to diet and exercise instead.'

4. Read *Parents 'are scared to talk to their children about weight issues'* on page 9. In small groups, discuss how parents could sensitively talk to their child about weight issues. Feedback to the rest of your class and compare notes.

Moral dilemma

5. Imagine you are the parent of a twelve-year-old girl who is extremely unhappy about her weight. Your daughter has tried diets and exercise but cannot seem to lose any weight. She has decided that she wants to have a gastric band fitted in order to lose weight. How would you handle this situation? Would you allow her to have the surgery?

Research activities

6. The National Trust has launched a campaign called *50 things to do before you are 11$^{3/4}$* to encourage sofa-bound children to be more active and engage with the outdoors. Visit www.50things.org.uk. Have you done any of these 50 things already? Which would you like to do next? Think of some ideas that you could add to the list and discuss this with your class.

7. Research Sainsbury's *Active Kids* campaign and write a summary for your local newspaper.

Written activity

8. Read the article *Obese children to be put up for adoption* on page 5. Do you agree or disagree with social workers' decision to remove the children from their parents' care? Write a letter to *The Telegraph* voicing your opinion.

Design activity

9. Choose an article from this chapter and create an illustration to accompany it.

Start active, stay active

This article has been adapted from the guidelines issued by the four Chief Medical Officers (CMOs) of England, Scotland, Wales and Northern Ireland.

Evidence shows that we should all aim to take part in some kind of physical activity; even small increases in physical activity can help to protect us against diseases and improve our happiness and well-being.

The amount, and type, of activity we should do depends on our age.

Children under five-years-old

Physical activity should be encouraged from a very young age, even in babies and young children. To keep babies active, parents can encourage safe floor or water based play.

When a child is old enough to walk without help, they should be physically active for at least 180 minutes every day. These minutes can be spread throughout the day.

Children and young people (five- to 18-years-old)

All children and young people should be physically active for between 60 minutes and several hours every day. Activity can be moderate or intense. Intense activities strengthen muscles and bones, and should be included at least three days a week.

Adults (19- to 64-years-old)

Adults should try to be active every day. Over a week, they should do at least 150 minutes (two and a half hours) of activity; this can be in sets of 10 minutes, or more. One way to do this would be to complete 30 minutes activity on five days of the week. Intense activity to strengthen muscle and bone should be included at least two days a week.

Older adults (65+ years)

Any kind of physical activity that older adults do will help them to stay healthy. They should try to be active daily, and complete at least 150 minutes of moderate activity every week.

Older adults should include physical activity that will improve balance and coordination on at least two days every week, to combat their risk of falls. They should also include activities that help muscle strength on at least two days every week.

11 July 2011

The above information is adapted from the Start Active, Stay Active report issued by the four Chief Medical Officers (CMOs) of England, Scotland, Wales and Northern Ireland. © Crown Copyright 2011

www.bhfactive.org.uk

Mini glossary

Activity of moderate intensity – feels quite hard; your breath will get quicker and you will start to sweat after about 10 minutes.

Activity of vigorous intensity – feels very challenging; you will be very out-of-breath, and start to sweat after just a couple of minutes.

Tip – a good way to test whether you are doing moderate or vigorous exercise, is to see if you can have a conversation with a friend while you are doing it. If you can chat easily, this is moderate exercise. If you are too out of breath to chat, this is vigorous exercise.

Pause for thought...

➤ **What kind of physical activity do you think is appropriate for children under five years old? What would you recommend to a parent who wanted to make sure their toddler was active?**

Half of people in UK cannot run 100 metres

New research by YouGov for Slimming World shows nearly half of adults cannot run 100 metres.

A survey has found that nearly half of adults in the UK (45%) think it would be difficult or impossible to run 100 metres without stopping.

The survey was conducted to mark the start of Slimming World's 'Miles for Smiles' activity programme. The programme will encourage people to become more active while raising money for the NSPCC at the same time.

2,065 people were asked about their weight, eating habits and fitness levels and the survey found that:

➤ Women are almost twice as likely as men to be brought out in a cold sweat by the idea of running 100 metres, with 56% of women believing it would be difficult or impossible to run the distance compared to 31% of men.

➤ Three out of four people (75%) in the UK never take part in competitive activity and more than half (55 %) never take part in non-competitive activity either.

➤ Six out of ten men (59%) enjoy watching sport on TV at least once a week, with that figure likely to have risen during the Olympic season.

Carolyn Pallister, Slimming World's public health manager, said:

'These findings show how daunting the idea of physical activity can be for the many of us who lead completely sedentary lives. It's easy to fall out of the habit of being active and the longer we go without doing it the less confident we feel. For people who are worried about their weight or poor fitness – and that's the majority of the population – the thought of taking those first steps to a more active lifestyle can feel terrifying and, with busy lives, it's easy to make excuses and decide that now just isn't the right time to make a change.

Pallister said she hoped that the rise in sport spectators in London's 2012 Olympic Games would lead to a rise in physical activity; however, she does concede that watching world class athletes could make people feel less capable of being active themselves.

'The real focus of any programme designed to help people become more active needs to be about helping people to build their confidence in their ability to make changes,' she said. 'Being encouraged to start slowly and find ways of being active that they enjoy and can build into their everyday life can help take the threat out of activity.

At Slimming World they find that helping members to identify ways of moving more, and supporting them to increase their activity levels gradually, can grow their confidence as they build up to a more active lifestyle.

'Whether it's taking the stairs instead of the lift, swapping sedentary video consoles for active gaming like the Nintendo Wii or Xbox Kinect or trading nights in front of the TV for more active pursuits like taking a brisk walk, joining a zumba class or kicking a football around in the park, we see firsthand what a difference small, enjoyable changes can make.'

6 August 2012

www.yougov.co.uk

Fitness training tips

It's important to exercise safely and effectively. Robin Gargrave of YMCAfit, one of the UK's top trainers of fitness professionals, shares his tips on getting into shape safely.

When should I exercise?

There's no right time to exercise. It depends on the individual. 'You need to listen to your body,' says Robin. 'Some people feel rough in the morning, whereas others can hop out of bed and do a ten mile run.'

Don't exercise for two to three hours after a heavy meal. If you exercise straight after a large meal, you're likely to experience nausea, stomach cramps and discomfort.

Recommended physical activity levels

- Children under five years old should do 180 minutes every day.
- Young people (five to 18-years-old) should do 60 minutes every day.
- Adults (19- to 64-years-old) should do 150 minutes every week.

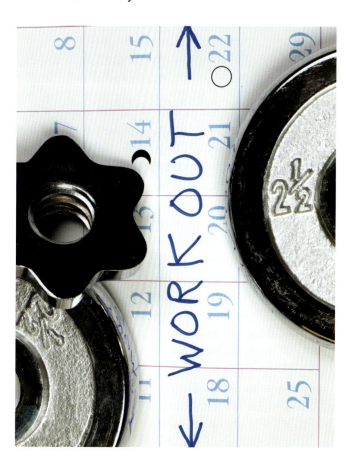

- Older adults (65 and over) should do 150 minutes every week.

Can I have a snack before exercising?

You can have a small snack before your workout, such as a piece of fruit or a drink. Robin advises against snacks that are high in sugar, including soft drinks.

'You might get a quick energy boost but it'll probably be followed by a sudden energy slump.' Choose starchy foods, such as brown bread or bananas, which help keep your energy levels constant during exercise.

Should I warm up before exercise?

Warming up is essential before exercising. 'Without a warm-up, your workout won't be as efficient as it could be,' says Robin. 'Your muscles won't be warm and will be less supple, which can increase your risk of injury.'

Start with slow, gentle movements, such as walking, and gradually build the intensity, such increasing your walking pace to a gentle jog.

Eight to ten minutes will warm up the muscles and get them ready for higher-intensity activity. The warm-up process sends oxygen to the muscles, where it works with glucose to produce energy, Robin says. This ensures that the body works more efficiently, and that your workout gives better results.

What is aerobic activity?

Aerobic activity is any activity where the body's large muscles move in a rhythmic manner for a continuous period of time. Also called endurance activity, it's great for improving the health of your heart and lungs. Examples include:

➢ running
➢ walking
➢ cycling
➢ swimming.

'Aerobic activity is vital for burning off calories, weight management and general health,' says Robin.

What's the importance of strength training?

Strength-training activities, such as weight lifting, involve short bursts of effort. Strength training burns calories and builds and strengthens muscle. Benefits of strength training include increasing bone density, strengthening joints and improving balance, stability and posture.

'It increases your ability to do everyday tasks without getting so tired,' says Robin. 'The more muscle mass you have, the easier it is to burn calories, even when the body is at rest.'

Do I need to stretch?

Stretching helps to improve flexibility, balance and posture. To stretch properly and safely, slowly stretch the muscle just until you feel resistance. Resistance is the point at which you feel a slight pull. It should not be painful. Stop and hold each stretch for ten to 20 seconds without bouncing up and down.

During the stretch, breathe deeply and regularly. Don't hold your breath. Make sure your muscles are warmed up before you stretch. The best time to stretch is after exercise, when your muscles are most supple.

What's the importance of cooling down?

Immediately after your workout, take time to cool down. This gradually lowers your heart rate and allows your body to recover. It may help reduce muscle injury, stiffness and soreness. Walk or continue your activity at a low intensity for five to ten minutes. It's then an ideal time to stretch, and you're more likely to improve your flexibility.

Should I have a rest day?

With moderate-intensity aerobic activity, whether it's heavy gardening or cycling, you're encouraged to do a little every day. Adults should do 150 minutes (two hours and 30 minutes) of moderate-intensity aerobic activity a week. Children aged five to 18 should do 60 minutes of moderate to vigorous aerobic activity every day.

It's important to rest when you do vigorous-intensity aerobic activity, such as running. The body repairs and strengthens itself between workouts, and over-training can weaken even the strongest athletes.

What should I drink?

It's important to drink fluid during any exercise that lasts for more than 30 minutes.

Water may be enough for low-intensity exercise up to 45–50 minutes.

For higher-intensity exercise of 45–50 minutes or more, or lower-intensity exercise lasting several hours, a sports drink can help maintain energy levels and its salt will improve hydration. Choose drinks that contain sodium (salt) when exercise lasts longer than one hour, or in any event when large amounts of salt will be lost through your sweat.

How do I stay motivated?

Make sure your exercise regime includes activities that you like doing rather than what someone else tells you to do. Exercise with a friend or friends so that you can all keep each other motivated.

'Set new challenges to keep yourself stimulated,' says Robin. 'And keep going. It's always hard at first, even for elite athletes, but it does get easier.'

16 July 2011

'How I caught the running bug'

Aimee Albert talks about starting running, running to music and sharing her running goals on Facebook.

When did you first start running?

I started running about a month ago. I've never been any good at sport. As a child, I had mobility problems because of weak ankles and knees and that really held me back. I'd always thought 'I can't do sport'. But I just knew I had to start leading a healthier life while I was still young. I started doing exercises to strengthen my legs and then felt I could take it a bit further. I considered joining a gym but that's expensive so I decided to give running a go. Anyone can run. All you need is a pair of running shoes.

How did you get started?

I did a bit of research on running shoes. I spoke to friends who were runners and looked at websites like Runner's World. I was advised to go to a specialist running shop, where staff are trained to analyse your running style and help you choose the right pair of shoes. My local store had a treadmill, where they filmed me running to look at how my foot strikes the ground. They recommended some shoes – they're really comfy.

The next step was to search for music. I knew I didn't want to run with other people. I just wanted to get on with it by myself. I liked the idea of running to music and I was told you could get music specifically for running. I found the AudioFuel tracks on iTunes and bought Easy Beats, which is a gentle 30-minute walk and jog session with voiceover coaching.

Before setting off, I worked out my route using the Mapmyrun website so that I'd be home by the end of my session.

Describe your progress since you starting running

Over the last month it's been great to find it less and less of a struggle to complete my 30-minute walking and jogging session. I've enjoyed it a lot more than I expected

right from the start. I had a few aches in my legs after my runs in the beginning. That's normal but it doesn't last. I've definitely caught the running bug. Now I'm looking forward to making more progress. I want to run for longer although not necessarily faster.

How has running with music helped?

AudioFuel produce music to match your foot stride to the beat as you run. Running to the beat makes it easy to keep to the right pace and not tire myself out too quickly by setting off too fast. It's a nice feeling to be able to complete a 30-minute run. I didn't think I'd like the coaching. I thought it would be intrusive but it really works. I like the encouraging words and the timekeeping. It doesn't feel intrusive at all. It just keeps you motivated and focused.

How do you feel since starting running?

I don't get tired so much anymore. I now manage to run for the full half hour. I used to reach certain points on my run where I'd feel exhausted and want to stop but now I just keep going. I don't feel like stopping. I can see my progress.

I feel much better about myself now. I've taken action to improve my fitness. I've overcome my struggle with doing sport. Having always said to myself 'I can't', I'm now actually doing it, and I'm not bad at it which has been a real feelgood factor for me. I'm feeling fitter and more energetic.

Running's also really good for stress. When you go out for a run it all drops away and you stop feeling cross or worried. I don't care what I look like. I've lost my self-consciousness. Everyone looks hot and sweaty so it doesn't matter.

How do you fit running into your routine?

I like running in the evening. I'm not really a morning person. I tend to come home from work, put my shoes on and get out there. That's at around 6.30pm. It relaxes me after work and then I can have a nice relaxing bath afterwards.

Have you set yourself any goals?

I've signed up to do a 5km charity run with my sister-in-law. It's a Race for Life event to raise money for Cancer Research UK. I've got people sponsoring me. It's great to have a goal. It keeps me on track with my running every week because I can't let people down. But it's not high pressure – there's people of every fitness level who enter. On the day, I can walk, jog or run.

Any tips for new runners?

Get a good pair of shoes so you avoid injury. Then just get on and do it. It was raining on the day of my first run, and I just got on with it. Plan your runs at the start of each week and try to stick to a routine. Tell people you're going for a run today – your partner or your Facebook friends – then you can't get out of it. There are days when you'd rather collapse on the sofa with a cup of tea. Try to blank out those thoughts. Just put on some feelgood music while you get ready. Don't think about it too much and get on with it.

31 May 2012

The above information is reprinted with kind permission from NHS Choices.
© NHS Choices 2012

www.nhs.uk

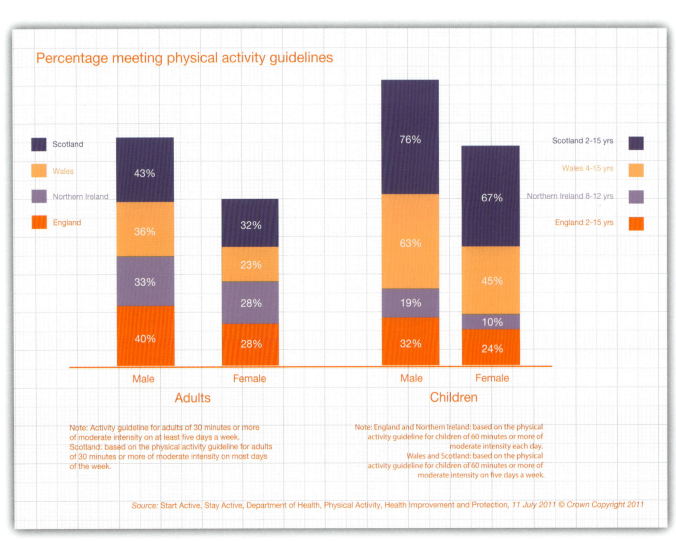

Percentage meeting physical activity guidelines

Scotland
Wales
Northern Ireland
England

Scotland 2-15 yrs
Wales 4-15 yrs
Northern Ireland 8-12 yrs
England 2-15 yrs

Adults
Male: 43%, 36%, 33%, 40%
Female: 32%, 23%, 28%, 28%

Children
Male: 76%, 63%, 19%, 32%
Female: 67%, 45%, 10%, 24%

Note: Activity guideline for adults of 30 minutes or more of moderate intensity on at least five days a week.
Scotland: based on the physical activity guideline for adults of 30 minutes or more of moderate intensity on most days of the week.

Note: England and Northern Ireland: based on the physical activity guideline for children of 60 minutes or more of moderate intensity each day.
Wales and Scotland: based on the physical activity guideline for children of 60 minutes or more of moderate intensity on five days a week.

Source: Start Active, Stay Active, Department of Health, Physical Activity, Health Improvement and Protection, *11 July 2011* © Crown Copyright 2011

Zombie fitness app a runaway success for UK business

A British-made fitness game – Zombies, Run! – has become a worldwide hit, getting players from across the globe running away from 'zombies' to get fit and reaching number 14 on the list of Top Grossing Apps worldwide.

Zombies, Run!, the brainchild of London-based games company Six to Start and writer Naomi Alderman, is the first ever fitness game with a story, and is becoming a huge hit with joggers from Italy to Australia. The game, downloaded as an app and played on iPhone or iPod, puts the player in the centre of a zombie apocalypse. Through their headphones, the player can hear zombies chasing them – and receives instructions to run in the real world to escape from them.

The app has already being called a breakthrough innovation in fitness and gaming, putting the player at the heart of the story. The player is called 'Runner Five', who comes from a tiny base which is the last remnant of humanity after the zombie apocalypse. Every time the player goes out running in the real world, they collect virtual 'supplies' such as batteries, water and canned food for their community.

The player has to run frequently to keep the base growing, and at the end of each run, they can decide how to allocate the batteries, bottled water or canned food. And the more they run, the more they discover about the dark backstory: how did the zombie apocalypse happen? Is there any hope for a vaccine? What is Runner Five's secret mission?

Since its launch on the iTunes App Store in late February, Zombies, Run! players have racked up 25 years spent running in the real world – that's over 200,000 hours or half a million miles, the distance to the Moon and back. Sales are expected to reach 100,000 copies soon.

Adrian Hon, CEO and co-founder of Six to Start says: 'I'm a keen runner and I wanted to create a game that would enhance the running experience. With Zombies, Run! you can run anywhere: city streets, parks, the beach, running trails, even on a treadmill, because our game measures how much you move as well as tracking the distance you run in the physical world. We've had literally thousands of emails, reviews and tweets from players telling us how we've motivated them to run further and faster than before – all the way from kids aged 12 to grandparents aged 65.'

Naomi Alderman, lead writer on the project says: 'It's important to me that the game's open to walkers as well as runners – people who are just starting on a fitness journey. We're not going to penalise you for going slowly or demand you do your 'personal best' every time. We're just going to tell you an amazing story, where you get to be the hero of your own zombie apocalypse and so even when you don't really feel like getting out there you've got extra motivation to just put on your shoes and start.'

Zombies, Run! was created entirely by British developers, writers, artists, designers and actors, and with over 90% of sales outside the UK, it's a huge export success story. The game was funded using Kickstarter, a crowdfunding site where creative teams can help get projects off the ground by selling pre-orders and rewards. In September 2011, Zombies, Run! attracted $73,000 in pledges from 3,500 backers around the world.

For more information, visit www.zombiesrungame.com

For further enquiries, email press@zombiesrungame.com or call 033 3340 7490

3 April 2012

The above information is reprinted with kind permission from Nesta.
© Nesta 2012

www.nesta.org.uk

Mini glossary

Brainchild – *invention/idea.*

Key facts and figures

➢ Zombies, Run! reached number 14 on list of Top Grossing Apps worldwide

➢ It held the number 1 Top Grossing Health & Fitness Apps worldwide place for over two weeks

➢ It is still in the top 3 'Top Grossing Health & Fitness' Apps

➢ Sales close to 100,000 copies

➢ In just one month, players have spent 25 years running, or 200,000 hours – half a million miles

➢ Zombies, Run! can be played anywhere in the world, at any speed – from walking to jogging to running, and even on a treadmill

➢ The game will contain over 30 missions, each lasting 20-30 minutes long

➢ The app allows players to listen to their own music and playlists while running

➢ Distance, time, pace, are recorded for each run

➢ Custom mission packs will be available for purchase to help players train for races, along with options for cyclists

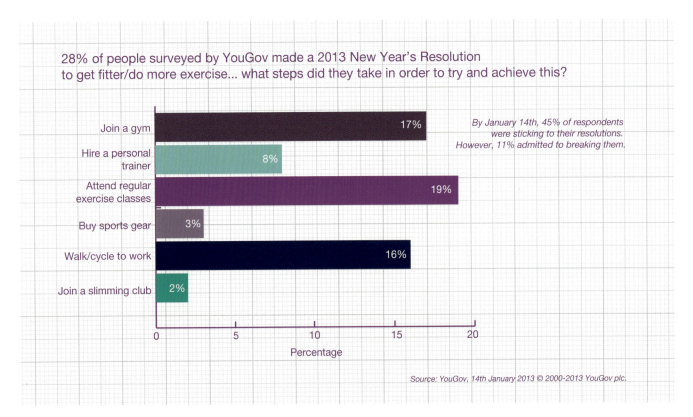

28% of people surveyed by YouGov made a 2013 New Year's Resolution to get fitter/do more exercise... what steps did they take in order to try and achieve this?

By January 14th, 45% of respondents were sticking to their resolutions. However, 11% admitted to breaking them.

Step	Percentage
Join a gym	17%
Hire a personal trainer	8%
Attend regular exercise classes	19%
Buy sports gear	3%
Walk/cycle to work	16%
Join a slimming club	2%

Source: YouGov, 14th January 2013 © 2000-2013 YouGov plc.

Outdoor fitness equipment: taking the 'play' out of the playground?

Recently there seems to have been an increase in the number of parks that have outdoor 'gyms', with more and more community parks sprouting pieces of specialised equipment designed to encourage adults to be active.

By Sally Pears

In theory, these 'adult playgrounds' sound like a great idea:

➤ They're free: for anyone put off by the cost of gym memberships or home equipment, free outdoor gyms are a great alternative.

➤ They're outside: perfect for anyone who doesn't have space at home to workout, or who wants to get out in the fresh air and maybe get some sun (not that we've had much of that here in the UK lately).

➤ They're a good exercise reminder: acting as a prompt to anyone walking past that they should maybe get a little more exercise.

➤ They're inexpensive: As far as public health interventions, outdoor gyms are relatively cheap – there's a one-off payment for the equipment and that's it – no fees for staff, no printing/advertising costs, etc.

BUT, how effective are these outdoor gyms in practice, really? Personally, I think there are a number of reasons why investing public money in outdoor fitness equipment isn't the best idea:

1. No privacy

For anyone wanting to get fitter/get in shape, an outdoor gym probably comes a close second to donning a swimsuit in terms of potential for embarrassment. Many people often claim that they dislike gyms because they feel embarrassed about working out in public, so working out in a community park (surrounded by children, teenagers, dog walkers, etc.) would probably not be a good alternative!

2. No instruction

Again, for anyone starting out, these workout spaces provide very little instruction about how to use the equipment. Sure, each piece of kit may come with a sign explaining how to use it and what it's good for (e.g. cardiovascular conditioning, leg strength, balance, etc.) but there's rarely any information about how to put everything together – for example, how long should you do each exercise for, how many exercises should you do in one session, how often should you do the exercises. This might seem to take the 'fun' out of using the equipment, but another barrier to exercise often cited by people is that they don't know what to do! Providing free equipment is therefore only one half of the solution.

3. They just make no sense!

Okay, so this is my biggest argument against these outdoor 'gyms'. Most of the ones that I have seen have at least one or two pieces of equipment that are designed to mimic the 'cardio' machines found in fitness centres. Now, call me crazy, but surely you have to question the sense of producing specialised outdoor equipment that mimics gym equipment...which was itself originally designed to mimic the kind of activities that people do outdoors! For example:

- An outdoor 'treadmill' (i.e. steel rollers that you 'run' on) mimics an indoor treadmill which mimics walking or running!
- An outdoor stationary bike mimics an indoor stationary bike which mimics cycling!
- An 'air walker' mimics the beloved cross-trainer which mimics… well, I never really have managed to figure out what movement a cross-trainer is designed to imitate!

I mean, come on! You're in a PARK! If you want to encourage people to exercise, what about providing them with actual bikes? Or setting up a walking or running group? Or even a setting up a frisbee golf course?!

Now, okay, some of you may agree that providing outdoor cardio equipment might not be the best idea, but surely there's a place for outdoor resistance machines like a shoulder press, chest press or leg press?

Well, I don't know if you've ever come across any outdoor resistance machines, but on the whole they actually offer very little actual 'resistance', mainly because it's tricky to provide an adjustable outdoor machine which won't rust excessively or need regular maintenance, but also because it's generally considered unsafe to provide heavy weights to the (unsupervised) general public. So, given that the 'resistance' machines don't actually offer much resistance, why not just encourage people to use their own bodyweight instead:

- Chest Press? – Why not a push up?
- Shoulder Press? – Why not a pike push up?
- Leg Press? – Why not a squat?

The same goes for machines like the 'twist plate' that are designed to improve hip mobility – what about good, old-fashioned hip circles? Or multi-planar lunges?

The solution?

I really do appreciate that councils are trying to encourage people to be more physically active and I definitely think that money invested in physical activity promotion/interventions could bring significant savings in terms of NHS costs. However, I think that money spent on outdoor cardio equipment and resistance machines is just a waste of resources. But what's the alternative?

Personally, I would love to see some money spent on creating outdoor 'gyms' for adults which not only provide areas and advice on bodyweight exercises, but that also put the 'play' back into 'playgrounds' with balance beams, monkey bars, cargo nets and zip wires!

What are your thoughts on this issue and what physical activity promotion programmes do YOU think would be a good idea?

23 October 2012

www.fitnessnewspaper.com

New research shows that healthy teenagers are happy teenagers

Research into adolescent health behaviour by Dr Cara Brooks used information from *Understanding Society*, a long-term study of 40,000 UK households. The study was funded by the Economic and Social Research Council (ESRC).

Dr Brooks looked at the responses of 5,000 young people, aged ten to 15, to questions about their health-related behaviours and levels of happiness. The results show that:

- Young people who never drank any alcohol were between four and six times more likely to have higher levels of happiness than those who reported any alcohol consumption.
- Young people who smoked were about five times less likely to have high happiness scores compared to those who never smoked.
- Eating more fruit and vegetables and eating less crisps, sweets and fizzy drinks were both associated with high happiness.
- The more hours of sport young people participated in per week, the happier they were.

Researchers at the Institute for Social and Economic Research at the University of Essex believe the data shows that unhealthy behaviours such as smoking, drinking alcohol and taking no exercise are closely linked to substantially lower happiness scores among teenagers, even when factors such as gender, age, family income and parent's education are taken into account.

The researchers argue that 'there are clear long-term links between health-related behaviours and well-being in adulthood. Helping young people to reduce damaging health choices as they start making independent decisions is important in order to reduce the number of adults at risk from chronic disease because of their low well-being and poor health-related behaviours.'

The PSHE Association believes that this research is important for schools to understand and continues to press for PSHE education to be made mandatory for all children and young people in schools taught by properly trained, confident and competent teachers.

The findings above are taken from the article 'Happiness and health-related behaviours in adolescence' from the *Understanding Society: Findings 2012* report.

5 March 2012

The above information is reprinted with kind permission from the PSHE Association. © PSHE Association 2012

www.pshe-association.org.uk

Young women and girls' physical activity

This factsheet summarises the recent key findings around young women and girls' participation in sport and physical activity.

Main findings:

Just a quarter of girls meet current recommended levels of physical activity a week.

Female drop off in sport starts even earlier than males.

Despite PE being compulsory in schools, one in five girls still does no activity in a week.

For girls, being fit and healthy is the most popular reason for taking part in PE/sport. Other motivations include working as a team, making friends, being considerate and helping them to think about others.

Girls think sports traditionally played by boys, such as rugby and football, are seen to be more important than sports played by girls.

Recommended levels of physical activity

- ➢ Just a quarter of girls take part in 60 minutes of physical activity every day, compared with a third of boys.
- ➢ The proportion of girls taking part in the recommended levels of activity a week declines with age, particularly after the age of ten.

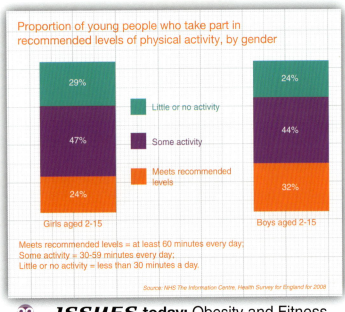

Proportion of young people who take part in recommended levels of physical activity, by gender

Girls aged 2-15: 29% Little or no activity; 47% Some activity; 24% Meets recommended levels

Boys aged 2-15: 24% Little or no activity; 44% Some activity; 32% Meets recommended levels

Meets recommended levels = at least 60 minutes every day;
Some activity = 30-59 minutes every day;
Little or no activity = less than 30 minutes a day.

Source: NHS The Information Centre, Health Survey for England for 2008

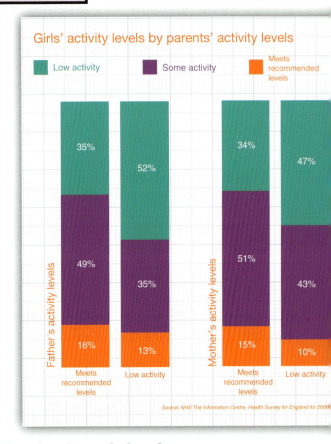

Girls' activity levels by parents' activity levels

Low activity | Some activity | Meets recommended levels

Father's activity levels:
- Meets recommended levels: 35% Low activity, 49% Some activity, 16% Meets recommended levels
- Low activity: 52% Low activity, 35% Some activity, 13% Meets recommended levels

Mother's activity levels:
- Meets recommended levels: 34% Low activity, 51% Some activity, 15% Meets recommended levels
- Low activity: 47% Low activity, 43% Some activity, 10% Meets recommended levels

Source: NHS The Information Centre, Health Survey for England for 2008

Physical activity by age

- ➢ By 15, half as many girls as boys are doing the recommended levels of activity.
- ➢ Girls' interest in informal sport (and games) declines more rapidly than formal sport.
- ➢ Girls are less likely to have low activity levels if their parents are active.

Organised sport

- ➢ Girls are less likely than boys to take part in any organised sport a week – 73% compared with 80%. The greatest differences between the sexes occur from age 13 onwards.
- ➢ Female drop off in sport starts earlier than males' – beginning at age 9–12 compared with age 13–16.
- ➢ One in six girls achieve five or more hours of activity a week (inside and outside of school) compared with one in four boys.

School provision of physical activity

➢ Almost three in five boys take part in three or more hours of high quality PE and out of schools sports in a week, compared with just over half of girls.

➢ The smallest differences by gender are in years one to seven. The gap between the sexes widens as pupils get older until, by Year 13, the difference is 13 percentage points.

➢ Overall, 78% of girls in years 1–13 participate in at least 120 minutes of curriculum PE, compared with 80% of boys. It looks like there is very little difference overall, and this is true for every year group in primary school. However, on entry to secondary school a difference in participation levels by gender starts, rising to four or five percentage point differential in years ten to 13.

➢ Athletics, football and dance are the three most commonly offered sports at secondary school for girls.

➢ Sports more likely to be offered to girls than boys include dance, gymnastics, rounders, netball, hockey, trampolining, cheerleading, yoga and equestrian.

➢ Sports more likely to be offered to boys than girls include cricket, basketball, rugby, golf, table tennis, softball, boxing and baseball.

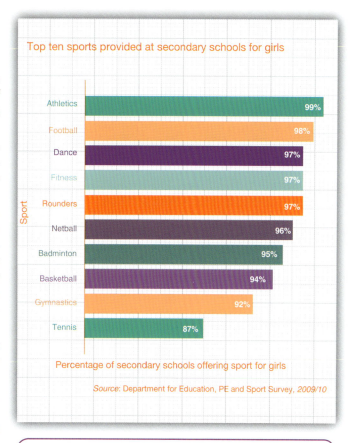

Top ten sports provided at secondary schools for girls

Sport	Percentage of secondary schools offering sport for girls
Athletics	99%
Football	98%
Dance	97%
Fitness	97%
Rounders	97%
Netball	96%
Badminton	95%
Basketball	94%
Gymnastics	92%
Tennis	87%

Source: Department for Education, PE and Sport Survey, *2009/10*

The above information is reprinted with kind permission from the Women's Sport and Fitness Foundation report Young women and girls' physical activity: December 2010 © Women's Sport and Fitness Foundation 2010

www.wsff.org.uk

American sisters, aged eight and nine, start their own fitness class

Alyssa and Makayla Esparza, aged eight and nine, are fed up with being overweight. The sisters from San Antonio, Texas know they are not as healthy as they could be and have challenged themselves to stick to a healthy-living regime for at least 90 days. Their fitness routine involves playing Dance Central, walking their dogs and riding their bikes, but they don't just want to improve their own fitness; Alyssa and Makayla would like their whole neighbourhood to get involved, so they have placed an ad on Craigslist:

> Kids needed for a healthy and active kid programme, started by a kid
>
> We need kid volunteers who want to be more active and eat healthy!

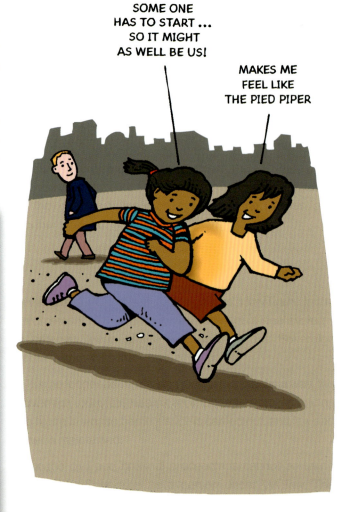

SOME ONE HAS TO START ... SO IT MIGHT AS WELL BE US!

MAKES ME FEEL LIKE THE PIED PIPER

'A lot of kids don't have someone telling them what to do, or what to eat. So, if they can take it upon themselves and they know what to do, they might go for the healthier snacks, rather than the junk food.'

Alyssa hopes that exercising as a group will be key to their success, 'Because it's like, they're supporting me, I'm supporting them. It's better for people to be with you, instead of just alone in the programme' and Makayla says that if the program helped 'just one person who was overweight, and they could keep on doing this, it would be super great!'

5 February 2013

The Esparza sisters aim for their healthy-living kids' group to meet two or three times a week, to exercise together and learn about healthy food choices. The girls' grandmother, Dawn Guerrero, believes that if children are given the tools to understand fitness and diet, they are more likely to make the right choices and feel in control:

Fitness advice for wheelchair users

If you're a wheelchair user, it can be easy to overlook physical fitness and exercise. But getting active will bring you important health benefits and can help you manage daily life, too.

Wheelchair users can face particular challenges when it comes to fitness and exercise.

But regular aerobic exercise – the kind that raises your heart rate and causes you to break a sweat – and muscle-strengthening exercise are just as important for the health and wellbeing of wheelchair users as they are for other adults.

Whatever your preferences and level of physical ability, there will be options that are right for you.

Physical activity doesn't have to mean the gym, or competitive sport, though these can be great options. Activity can take many forms, and happen in many places.

Why you should get active

Regular physical activity is good for physical and mental wellbeing, and can be a great way to meet new people.

Philip Gill is a specialist tutor at YMCAfit, an organisation that trains fitness professionals. He specialises in training fitness professionals who work with wheelchair users and people with other disabilities.

'The repeated pushing motion that is used to push a wheelchair means that the chest and shoulder muscles can become tight and prone to injury. Meanwhile the back muscles can become weaker, because they are never worked'

He says that getting active is important for wheelchair users for a range of reasons: 'Using a wheelchair can make it more difficult to do physical activity that raises your heart rate and makes you warm enough to break a sweat. This kind of exercise is important for the health of your heart and lungs. Missing out on this kind of exercise can contribute to weight gain over time.

'Manoeuvring or pushing a wheelchair can also put particular strain on certain muscles in the upper body, making strains or other injuries more likely. Muscle-strengthening exercises can help you to manage your wheelchair in daily life, and avoid these kinds of injuries.'

How much activity?

The Department of Health says adults between the ages of 19 and 64 should do at least 150 minutes of moderate-level aerobic activity a week, and muscle-strengthening activity on two or more days a week.

If you're a wheelchair user, getting active regularly will bring you important health benefits.

Philip Gill says these general guidelines can help wheelchair users, too: 'In the absence of specific guidelines, wheelchair users can compare their activity levels to the general guidelines for adults,' he says.

'Many wheelchair users will not be doing anywhere near that volume of physical activity. If that's you, then see these guidelines as a goal, which you should take small steps towards.

'Remember: even small increases in physical activity will bring health benefits.'

What kind of activity?

Philip Gill says the kinds of physical activity that are right for you depend on your level of physical ability, and the types of activity that appeal to you.

'Your aim might be to improve certain aspects of physical function, to help with daily life. Or you may be seeking improved fitness, or involvement in competitive sport,' he says.

'Whatever your level of physical ability and confidence, there are activities you can do to improve fitness.'

Cardiovascular exercise

There are a range of options available for taking cardiovascular exercise in a wheelchair.

'The aim is to raise your heart rate, and be warm enough to break a sweat,' says Gill. 'You should be slightly out of breath: enough that you can still hold a conversation, but not sing the words of a song.

'If you're unused to exercise or you haven't exercised for some time, aim to start with 10-minute sessions, and gradually build up towards 20 minutes.'

Gill suggests these ideas:

- ➤ swimming
- ➤ wheelchair sprinting, in a studio or at a track
- ➤ using a rowing machine adapted for wheelchair use
- ➤ wheelchair sports, such as basketball, netball and badminton
- ➤ muscle-strengthening exercise.

When it comes to muscle-strengthening exercise, Philip Gill says you should pay special attention to certain muscle groups.

'The repeated pushing motion that is used to push a wheelchair means that the chest and shoulder muscles can become tight and prone to injury. Meanwhile the back muscles, which are not involved in this pushing motion, can become weaker, because they are never worked.

'Because of this, it's a good idea to focus on exercises that work the smaller muscles that support the pushing motion, such as the shoulder muscles: this can help prevent injury. You can also strengthen the back muscles by doing exercises that involve a pulling motion.'

Gyms with equipment adapted for wheelchair users are a great place to do muscle-strengthening activities.

Some wheelchair users also find that they can do muscle-strengthening exercises at home, using resistance bands.

Get started

There are various ways to learn more about activities that are right for you, and find local facilities.

Parasport is an organisation dedicated to helping disabled people get involved in sports. Use the Parasport self-assessment wizard to find sports that are right for you.

The English Federation of Disability Sport runs the Inclusive Fitness Initiative, a scheme that ensures gyms are suitable for use by people with disabilities. Find a local IFI gym at the English Federation of Disability Sport website.

Your local recreation centre must ensure that it provides access to wheelchair users, according to the Disability Discrimination Act. If you have questions about your local recreation centre, such as what specialist equipment they have, or whether there are special sessions for wheelchair users, call ahead and ask.

8 March 2012

www.nhs.uk

Activities

Brainstorm

1. What is fitness?

2. Think of as many different kinds of physical activity as you can (e.g. swimming, walking, gardening). Then separate these activities into high, moderate and low intensity exercises.

Oral activities

3. With a partner, role play a situation in which one of you does very little physical activity and the other loves to exercise. The person who loves to exercise should try to persuade their friend that it can be fun and suggest ways they could get started.

4. In small groups, create a presentation that will persuade your local council to invest in an outdoor gym. Try using pictures, videos or demonstrations to engage your audience.

Research activities

5. Research a sport or fitness activity that you currently know very little about: the more obscure the better! Write some notes about your new sport, including the rules and any local facilities that are available. Feedback to your class.

6. Did you know that 'Half of people in the UK cannot run 100 metres'? Run 100 metres and time how long it takes you. What level of phyiscal activity do you think you felt while you were running? Low, moderate or high?

Written activities

7. Imagine that you are a PE teacher. You are worried that your students are not doing enough physical activity outside of school. Write a letter to your class' parents, explaining why physical activity is important and suggesting some easy and inexpensive things they could do to encourage their children to get fit.

8. Imagine that you are a teenage girl who hates taking part in PE at school. Write a blog post explaining your feelings and suggesting steps that teachers could take to make it more enjoyable.

Design activities

9. Read *Zombie fitness app a runaway success for UK business* on page 17. In groups, design a new fitness app that will encourage people to exercise. Your app should be fun and innovative!

10. Design a poster, that will be displayed in your school, promoting fitness for wheelchair users.

Key facts

- *Being obese can increase the risk of diseases such as type 2 diabetes, cancer and heart disease. (page 1)*

- *The latest Health Survey for England (HSE) data shows that in England in 2010: 62.8% of adults (aged 16 or over) were overweight or obese, 30.3% of children (aged 2-15) were overweight or obese and 26.1% of all adults and 16% of all children were obese. (page 1)*

- *It is estimated that obese and overweight people cost the NHS £5.1 billion per year. (page 1)*

- *A study has found that almost two thirds of UK adults are putting their health at risk through a lack of exercise. (page 3).*

- *Malta was the laziest country worldwide, with 72 per cent of adults classified as physically inactive, but Britain (63%) far outstretched other countries like the USA (41%), France (33%) and Greece (16%). (page 3)*

- *Physical inactivity was responsible for 5.3 million of the 57 million deaths worldwide in 2008 including six to ten per cent of cases of heart disease, type 2 diabetes, breast and colon cancer, they estimated. (page 3)*

- *Over a third of parents (37%) feel that talking to their child about their weight might lower their self-esteem. (page 9)*

- *Two thirds of parents (66%) said they'd like more support in talking to their child about weight. (page 9)*

- *The amount, and type, of activity we should do depends on our age. (page 11)*

- *A survey has found that nearly half of adults in the UK (45%) think it would be difficult or impossible to run 100 metres without stopping. (page 12)*

- *Three out of four people (75%) in the UK never take part in competitive activity and more than half (55 %) never take part in non-competitive activity either. (page 12)*

- *A British-made fitness game – Zombies, Run! – has become a worldwide hit and reached number 14 on the list of Top Grossing Apps worldwide. (page 17)*

- *For girls, being fit and healthy is the most popular reason for taking part in PE/sport. Other motivations include working as a team, making friends, being considerate and helping them to think about others. (page 22)*

- *Just a quarter of girls take part in 60 minutes of physical activity every day, compared with a third of boys. (page 22)*

- *Girls are less likely than boys to take part in any organised sport a week – 73% compared with 80%. The greatest differences between the sexes occurs from age 13 onwards. (page 22)*

Glossary

BMI (body mass index) *– BMI is used to measure a person's weight in relation to their height. If a person has a BMI below 18.5 they are classed as being underweight, a BMI of 25–29 is considered overweight and a BMI of 30 and over is obese.*

Exercise intensity *– This refers to how much energy use when you exercise. Exercise intensity can be broken down into light, moderate or vigorous:*

Light intensity feels easy; you have no noticeable changes in your breathing pattern and don't break a sweat.

Moderate intensity feels somewhat hard; your breath quickens and you develop a sweat after about ten minutes of activity (e.g. leisurely cycling, brisk walk, gardening).

Vigorous intensity feels very challenging; you can't carry on a conversation due to deep, rapid breathing and you develop a sweat after a few minutes of activity (e.g. jumping rope, basketball, running).

Fitness *– The condition of being physically healthy. A high level of fitness is usually the result of regular exercise and a proper nutritious diet.*

Obesity *– If a person has a BMI of 30 or over they are considered to be obese. This puts them at risk for a number of serious health problems, such as an increased risk of heart disease and type 2 diabetes. Worldwide obesity has more than doubled since 1980 and this is most likely due to our increasingly less active lifestyles.*

Weight loss surgery *– Weight loss surgery is used to help patients who have previously struggled to lose weight, and who are usually dangerously obese, to lose weight and keep it off. Weight loss surgery can provide a lasting solution for a wide range of obesity-related problems like diabetes or sleep apnoea. The most common weight loss surgery is a gastric band operation. This is where an elastic band is fitted across the top end of the stomach to restrict the amount of food the person can eat before feeling full. Weight loss surgery is a major medical procedure and shouldn't be viewed as a quick fix; patients must maintain a strict diet and exercise regime after having the procedure. After-care is also important, with the patient having to undergo an intensive treatment programme with a dietician and a psychologist.*